J

D1575549

JAN 13   KN
(9)

Big Bad Sheep

Big Bad Sheep

Written by
Bettina Wegenast

Illustrated by
Katharina Busshoff

Translated by
Helena Ragg-Kirkby

Eerdmans Books for Young Readers
Grand Rapids, Michigan • Cambridge, U.K.

Text © 2005 Bettina Wegenast
Illustrations © 2005 Katharina Busshoff
English language translation © 2012 Helena Ragg-Kirkby

Original title: *Wolf Sein*
First published © 2005 Patmos Verlagsgruppe
Sauerländer Verlag, Mannheim, Germany

This edition published 2012 in the United States of America by
Eerdmans Books for Young Readers,
an imprint of Wm. B. Eerdmans Publishing Co.
2140 Oak Industrial Dr. NE, Grand Rapids, Michigan 49505
P.O. Box 163, Cambridge CB3 9PU U.K.

www.eerdmans.com/youngreaders

Manufactured at Worzalla, Stevens Point, Wisconsin, USA,
in March 2012; first printing

12 13 14 15 16 17 18   8 7 6 5 4 3 2 1

Library of Congress Cataloging-in-Publication Data

Wegenast, Bettina, 1963-
[Wolf sein. English.]
Big bad sheep / by Bettina Wegenast; illustrated by Katharina Busshoff;
translation by Helena Ragg-Kirkby.
p. cm.
Summary: Unable to stand by and watch his friend Kalle become a
sheep in wolf's clothing when he gets the job of big bad wolf on a trial basis,
Locke, also a sheep, takes on the job of hunter to stop Kalle's madness.
ISBN 978-0-8028-5409-4
[1. Sheep — Fiction. 2. Wolves — Fiction. 3. Dwarfs — Fiction.
4. Humorous stories.] I. Busshoff, Katharina, ill. II. Ragg-Kirkby, Helena. III. Title.
PZ7.H85664Bi 2012
[Fic — dc23
2011040437

The publication of this book has been made possible with the
financial support of the Goethe Institut.

Thanks to Guy Krneta
— B.W.

Chapter 1

"The Wolf is dead, the Wolf is dead!" The Three Little Pigs sang the words loudly and tunelessly, but with enormous gusto. "The Wolf is dead!"

Several sheep were standing in the meadow, munching grass. Suddenly Locke stopped munching. "So what was he like?"

"Who?" Karl, the sheep who was standing across from him, used his tongue to dislodge a blade of grass that was stuck between his teeth. He was bigger and stronger than Locke.

"The Wolf!" Locke was becoming slightly agitated.

"What do you think he was like? Bad!"

"Really bad?"

"Of course." Karl knew what he was talking about. "That's the way wolves are."

Locke thought for a moment. "So are all wolves bad?"

"Of *course* all wolves are bad. And he's the baddest of them all. He wasn't the Big Bad Wolf for nothing."

"Not for nothing?" Locke asked in astonishment. "You mean he got paid for it?"

"Of course he got paid for it." Karl grinned. "What did you think? The Big Bad Wolf . . . that's bound to pay well."

Locke blew bits of fluffy wool off his face. "Oh . . . I wonder what he looked like? What do you think?"

Karl made a face and rolled his eyes. "Bad, of course! He looked bad . . . really bad, with red eyes and black fur, that's what he looked like, and horribly shaggy."

"Oh yes! And I'm sure his coat was completely matted. And he had sharp claws and sharp teeth." Locke was beginning to get into the topic.

"Definitely. And between his teeth . . . old bits of food," said Karl darkly. "The remains of his victims."

Locke felt his wool starting to stand on end.

Quickly, the pair plucked out a morsel of grass each and chewed.

"So what did he do?" asked Locke through a mouthful of grass.

"What do you think he did?" Karl used his hoof to scrape out a particularly juicy tuft. "He was bad. I imagine that gave him more than enough to do."

"Sure. But what happens when someone's bad? Do they . . . bite sheep's legs?" A shiver ran down Locke's spine.

"Bite sheep's legs? Of course they do," said Karl. "And they do worse than that."

"Worse?"

"Much worse."

"But what could be worse than that?"

"Well . . . that depends . . . but I don't like to think about it. Thank goodness he's dead."

The Little Pigs' singing gradually faded into the distance until it could no longer be heard at all.

"So did you know him?" Locke now asked hesitantly. Nothing would surprise him about Karl.

Karl, however, denied it. "My goodness, no. Do you think I'd be standing here having a cozy chat and munch with you if I'd known him?"

"But you saw him."

"Saw him? Well, um . . . no, not really — but I *almost* saw him."

"Almost? What do you mean, almost? Did you see him or not?"

Karl looked up. "I think I once knew someone who saw him. Yes, and then . . . then of course there's Erwin, who did his shopping for him sometimes."

Locke was speechless. "Shopping? For the Big Bad Wolf? But . . ."

Karl remained completely cool. "Of course. How do you think it would look if the Big Bad Wolf himself went marching into a store?"

"Okay, fair enough, but I thought he was really bad."

"Of course he was really bad. But you still need stuff, even if you're really bad."

"And this Erwin bought it for him. I see."

A bumblebee buzzed over their heads. Locke watched it until it disappeared into the high grass. "And what's going to happen now? I mean, now that the Wolf is dead?"

Karl spat out a lump of earth that had been clinging to a tuft of grass. "They're looking for a new one. The job's already been advertised."

"Advertised? But why? Surely everyone should just be glad that the old one's dead." Locke was baffled.

"Of course everyone's glad that the old one's dead. But we really can't get by without any Wolf at all. There's always one around. There has to be! I'll have you know it's a really difficult

job. Not a job for a bell-wearing sheep . . ." Karl looked rather contemptuously at the little bell that hung around Locke's neck and gave a faint ting-a-ling every time he moved. He stretched his neck out proudly. Karl didn't wear a bell. "I've been wondering whether to apply for the job myself."

Locke coughed; he could almost have choked. "But . . . you're not a wolf. You're a sheep!"

"So? The wolf suit comes with the job. And it should be easy enough to figure out my teeth." Karl tested out his theory by baring his yellow teeth.

"I'm just going to go down there and find out what's what. Why not? I'd love to be really bad for once. I'd liven the place up, let me tell you." He looked expectantly at Locke. "So? How about you? Are you coming with me?"

Locke didn't reply. He looked up at the sky, where a heavy cloud was passing above them, casting its shadow onto the meadow.

"Are you coming?" Karl wasn't giving up so easily.

But Locke shook his head. Going with Karl to apply then and there for the Wolf's job? Did Karl think he was crazy?

"Come on, don't make such a fuss. What are you going to do? Spend your whole life standing in a meadow eating grass? End up as a leg of mutton? You can't be serious."

"I'm not a leg of mutton. I'm Locke!" Locke was insulted.

But that didn't bother Karl. "Once you're lying in slices on a plate, nobody's going to ask you what your name used to be. Come on, it's your chance too. And anyway, you'd enjoy it — I know you." His voice was as sweet as sugar. "Come on, Locke. We're a team, aren't we?"

Locke finally accepted defeat.

"Okay. If you're serious . . . You as the Big Bad Wolf — that's something I'd dearly love to see. Can't really imagine it though . . ." He took a deep breath. "I suppose I could do your shopping sometimes."

"Brilliant!" Karl was thrilled. "Come on, let's go straight down there. Not that anyone will beat us to it . . ." He jumped up and galloped across the meadow.

Locke took a last, longing look at the juicy grass before he trotted off after his friend.

Chapter 2

Karl stopped outside a nondescript little building. He looked around. "Here it is. The job center."

Nervously, he paced back and forth outside the door labeled "office."

"Don't you want to go in?" asked Locke.

"'Course I do. I can hardly wait." But Karl hesitated further. Then he suddenly pulled himself together and wrenched the door open.

"Hey! What sort of manners do you call that? I ask you!" snapped a disapproving voice.

It came from a little man in brown overalls and a pointy red hat who was sitting in a swivel chair behind a desk.

Karl planted himself before him, his legs apart.

"It's me," he said. "Me, the new Wolf."

It seemed to Locke as if his friend's familiar voice sounded deeper and somehow more threatening. But this didn't seem to impress the dwarf.

"Well, I never," he replied dismissively. "You want to be the new Wolf? Fine. But anyone can say that."

He busily shuffled the papers on the desk in front of him. "The position of Wolf has indeed just become available, that much is true. But as to whether you're suitable . . . we'll have to see about that." He stood up and came out from behind his desk. He studied Karl carefully. "We'll have to see about that . . ." he repeated.

"Go on, then. Looking doesn't cost anything."

The dwarf ran his fingers thoughtfully through his gray beard and straightened his hat. "We're not talking about external appearances. We can sort all that out. It's much more a question of inner values. Whether you're up to the job, for example."

Karl began pawing the ground uncomfortably under the dwarf's scrutinizing gaze. "My digestive system is in perfect working order. As are my teeth. But . . . would you mind opening the window a bit?"

The dwarf grinned broadly. "You're starting to feel a bit warm, are you?" He went over to the window and opened it a

Office

Wolf
Wanted

crack. "Is that better?" the dwarf asked, smiling again.

Locke, whom the dwarf had barely deigned to notice up to that point, didn't like this smile in the slightest. "He's due for a shearing," Locke said quickly. "His wool really is top notch. If you happened to be interested in a sweater . . . we've got excellent connections."

"Thanks, but no thanks. I don't need one. So let's get down to business." The dwarf turned to Karl again. "So why should we appoint you to the post of Wolf?"

"Because . . ." Karl looked at the ground.

"Well?" the dwarf drummed impatiently on his desk.

Karl took a deep breath. "Because . . . because I want it. Because I'm the best. Because I'm not one of those bell-wearing types. Because I want to know what the grass tastes like on the other side of the meadow. And because . . . let's face it, it pays well."

The dwarf stopped drumming. He looked at Karl in astonishment. Then he reverted to being cool and matter-of-fact once more. "Any other reasons?"

Karl stuck his chin out with great confidence. "And

because I'm always the best at *What time is it, Mr. Wolf?*" Now he was grinning broadly.

"*What time is it, Mr. Wolf?*" The dwarf frowned. "What's *What time is it, Mr. Wolf?* I've never heard of it."

"*What time is it, Mr. Wolf?* is a game," Locke explained. "And it's true: Karl's unbeatable as Mr. Wolf."

"So, it's a game . . . but this isn't a game," the dwarf said sternly.

Nothing was going to deter Karl. "I know. But you've got to have brains to be Mr. Wolf."

The dwarf now seemed amused. "So, you've got experience as Mr. Wolf. Good for you. Does that mean you can tell time as well?"

Karl hadn't been expecting that one. "Tell time? Do wolves have to be able to tell time?"

"Well, not necessarily, but if you've already worked as Mr. Wolf, you're bound to be able to tell time."

"Tell time . . . no . . . that is, not exactly. Mr. Wolf doesn't tell time in this game. He turns his face to the bushes."

Karl ducked down behind a chair. "The bushes have to have no thorns. You have to make sure of that. If you get stuck in them, you look pretty silly. So you hide there and wait. The lambs stand in the meadow, eating and playing. They have no idea what's up. But Mr. Wolf tenses every muscle and awaits his moment. And at the right moment . . ." Karl began to growl. He ducked down even lower. "Then . . . at the right moment: Dinner time! He jumps out. Pounces on the lambs."

Karl rushed out and was about to pounce on Locke when the dwarf quickly stepped out and stopped him in his tracks. "Thank you, that's fine, I get the picture."

Locke shook himself. "Brr . . . he's good, isn't he? It could really scare you . . . Yes, he was always the best at that. Phew . . ." He suddenly looked suspiciously at Karl. "When I see you like that . . . I almost think René was right. You really did bite him that time."

Karl pursed his lips contemptuously. "René? Nonsense. Stop talking about that sheep-brain. That show-off. That know-it-all. René, of all sheep!"

"But he said . . ."

"*René said!* I've had just about enough of him. Him and his bell! I'll tell you this: once I'm the Wolf, then we'll call on him. We'll pay him a real visit and . . ."

"If I might interrupt for a moment!" the dwarf intervened.

Karl quickly turned to him. "Of course. I'm sorry, we were just . . ."

"No worries. Your quarrels have nothing to do with me and, what's more, they don't interest me in the slightest." The dwarf was sitting back in his swivel chair, rocking gently back and forth. Then he fell silent and leaned nonchalantly on his desk. "And so far as your application is concerned . . . well . . . yes, I can see it. I guess we can give you a try."

Karl's eyes opened wide. "Yes? I've got the job? Really? I'm the Wolf? From now on, I'm the Wolf?"

Karl threw himself into position and began to growl. "I'm the Wolf!"

As Locke saw the sudden transformation in his friend, his

mouth gaped open. "Karl! Stop it!" he cried in horror.

The dwarf stood up again and walked in front of the desk. "Not bad. But calm down, please. Give you a try, I said. We'll give you a try. No more than that."

Karl's eyes narrowed to become little slits. "A try? Why only a try? I'm not a guinea pig, for goodness' sake."

The dwarf remained unimpressed. "That has nothing whatsoever to do with it. What it means is that we initially give you the job on probation. You get the opportunity to prove yourself as the Wolf. After a certain period, we review things and then decide whether to offer you a permanent position."

This was not what Karl had been expecting. "That's . . ."

He was about to protest, but the dwarf cut him off. "That's perfectly common, and in any case, you're not the only applicant."

"I'm not?" Karl was taken aback.

"No. Not by a long shot."

"Um . . . I thought . . . what's all that nonsense about

a probationary period? The job is made for me. And, while we're at it, you keep saying 'we.' So who are the others? Where are they hiding?" Karl looked around, searching.

"I'm part of a team," the dwarf explained grumpily. "Just a little cog in the wheel, so to speak. The others don't get involved in interviews; they prefer to remain in the background. So how about it? Do you want the job or not?"

"Of course I do. I'm not giving up that easily. So you want a sample of my work — well, you can have one. By the way, how long does this probation thing last?"

The dwarf rummaged in his papers. "Probation period for a Wolf . . . Aha, found it. Probationary period for a Wolf . . . well . . . shall we say the day after tomorrow? That should be long enough to see whether you're up to the job."

He pulled a large cardboard box off a shelf. "So. Here's your equipment. Better see whether it actually fits you." In the box was a tangled heap of black fur. He pulled it out and gave it a shake.

"First of all, the wolf suit." He coughed briefly and draped it over Karl's back. "Well, the fur's a bit dusty, but otherwise

it's in excellent condition."

He then tried to fit Karl into the coat, not entirely successfully. "If you could just pull your tummy in a bit . . ."

"That's not my tummy. I've just got a thick fleece," protested Karl.

"Well, if you could kindly just pull your thick fleece in a bit . . ." The dwarf finally took a step back and examined his handiwork. "Ah well. It'll do. Give it a day or two, and it'll fit you like a glove. And now . . . your teeth."

Karl pressed his lips together. "I don't need new teeth. There's nothing wrong with my teeth, thank you very much," he hissed.

The dwarf looked at him, amused. "I'm sorry, but you have no choice. The arrangement of a wolf's teeth is tried and true. If you don't mind . . ." With one quick movement he forced Karl's jaws apart, and just as rapidly shoved a set of razor-sharp teeth into his mouth.

"So, give me a growl."

"Grr . . ." Karl coughed and cleared his throat, then he tried a cautious growl. Quietly at first, then more loudly.

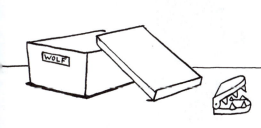

"Grrrrrrrrrrrrr!"

The dwarf seemed satisfied. "Well, that's pretty good. Now do a howl."

Karl cleared his throat. "Aooo!" he said.

"Not quite. Take a deep breath, open your mouth wide, and breathe out slowly."

Karl closed his eyes and took a deep breath. "Awowow . . ."

"Better already. Now imagine a dark night. Scraps of cloud are skimming across the sky. The full moon is casting its pale light on the earth . . ."

Karl took another deep breath, breathed out slowly, and this time it sounded like a proper wolf's howl. "Aoooowowow!"

A shiver ran down Locke's thick, fuzzy fleece. "Karl, stop it," he said pitifully. "You're scaring me."

"Fantastic," said the dwarf. "Go for it!"

"Aaaaoooooooooooooowowowowowowow!"

The dwarf was very impressed. "That really is very promising. You're a quick learner. Well, that's everything. We'll reconvene the day after tomorrow. In the meantime, you can have your first crack at being the Wolf. Show us what you're

made of."

Karl opened his eyes again. He cleared his throat. "And what about my salary? Is it actually worth my while? What about the terms and conditions? Personal insurance? Health insurance? Vacation?"

"Well . . . I don't think you'll have many complaints in that regard." The dwarf flicked through his papers again. "So . . . what does it say . . . We'll give you fifty hens, three little pigs, half a kingdom, and regular health exams. In particularly tricky situations we can also offer you psychological counseling. But someone like you — someone who's so wholehearted about the job — probably won't need to worry about that. It doesn't really go down well; it makes a bad impression on the public."

Karl frowned. "I can't see the point of it either. And all that other stuff — what am I supposed to do with that?"

"I beg your pardon? What do you mean?" The dwarf looked at him in astonishment.

"Hens. Pigs. I don't want to start a farm."

"You're not supposed to be starting a farm. You're a wolf,

for goodness' sake. And as for vacation . . . well, I have to tell you now that so far as we're concerned, there aren't any vacation days on the agenda. But you can choose how you spend your time. If you take a day off here and there . . . we would of course completely understand."

"Sounds good to me," said Locke, who had recovered from his fright and was eager to join in the conversation again. "You never go on vacation anyway. And all the other stuff . . . maybe you could sell it. Especially the half a kingdom. There's bound to be demand for that sort of thing."

"Yes indeed," confirmed the dwarf. "People always want hens and pigs too. But once you're a wolf, you might have something else in mind for them."

"And when will I be paid?" asked Karl. "Monthly?"

"What are you talking about?" The dwarf shook his head. "Of course not. We normally pay our employees at the end of their contract period."

"I beg your pardon?" Karl was furious. "Only at the end

of the job? That's fraud! What am I supposed to live on in the meantime?" He stamped his foot, threw his head back, and stared at the dwarf.

But the dwarf didn't flinch. "Oh, none of that's much use to you as a wolf anyway. It's much nicer if you can sit down in the twilight of your life and say: all this is mine. I earned it honestly. And in the meantime, you'll just live as wolves live. A morsel here, a tasty bite there . . ."

This, however, did not satisfy Karl.

"And what if I die before that? In an accident at work, say? That can happen, so I've heard. Then everything I've earned goes down the drain."

"Well . . ." the dwarf answered slowly. "You're right. But that's just the way it is. And in any case, it'll encourage you to be careful. If it's a problem for you, please just say so. As I said, we do have other applicants."

"No, no," said Karl quickly. "I didn't mean it like that."

"Then so far as I'm concerned, it's all set. You can choose where you want to start; there are numerous possibilities. Good luck! I look forward to a successful report. Goodbye, and have a nice day." The dwarf turned and started to rummage around on the shelves behind him.

The sheep looked at each other. Then Karl shrugged and left the room. Locke followed him.

Chapter 3

Outside, the sun was shining. Karl, sweltering inside his thick fur coat, trotted hastily toward the forest. Once in the shade of the trees, he sighed with relief and immediately began scratching his back against a mighty oak tree.

Then he went over to Locke and bared his teeth. "So? How do I look?" he asked.

Locke didn't reply right away. He had found a couple of juicy tufts of grass and was busily munching them.

"Hey! You!"

"Pardon?" Astonished, Locke looked up. "Are you talking to me?"

"Who else would I be talking to? How do I look?"

"Well . . ." Locke chewed and swallowed. "A bit out of the ordinary somehow . . . Not too bad, though."

"Not too bad? You call this 'not too bad'? I look fantastic!"

Karl scratched his back against the tree once more.

"Well, then . . . good for you! Seems a bit itchy, though."

"Oh, never mind a bit of itchiness. I barely notice it."

"Is that right? In that case, you must be scratching your back for some other reason. So what are we going to do now?"

"We? Why 'we'? What are *you* going to do now, is presumably what you meant to say."

"No, I didn't. I wanted to know what our plan is." Locke tugged at another tuft. This grass really was too good for words. He suddenly jumped.

"Grrrrrr . . ." Karl was behind him. "You heard me. The important thing is what *I'm* going to do. You just do as I say. I'm the Wolf now, and you're a sheep."

"Nonsense. You're a sheep, too," Locke protested. "I know you: you can't pull the wool over my eyes."

"You might be wrong there, my friend . . . What does my fur look like?"

"What do you think it looks like? Black and bristly, of course."

"What about my teeth? My eyes?"

"Your teeth are sharp and pointy, of course. Hey, Karl, what's all this about?"

Locke was starting to feel uncomfortable. Everything had gone so smoothly, and what was Karl doing? Instead of being pleased, he was putting on airs.

Karl persisted. "What are my eyes like?"

Karl's eyes? Locke looked at them closely. And he didn't like what he saw. "They're strange, somehow different," he said doubtfully. "Red . . . almost glowing, like coals. How on earth have you done that? Stop it — I don't like it."

"Stop it? Why should I? I've only just started. So: bristly black fur, sharp teeth, glowing eyes . . . ? That certainly doesn't sound like a sheep to me."

Locke looked at him in horror. "Nonsense. You're still a sheep. You might be wearing a wolf's clothing, but you're still a sheep. Karl! Wake up. You're a sheep!"

Karl grinned. The wolfish teeth glinted yellow in the sun. "Sheep . . . boring creatures . . . standing around in the grass, chomping away, with a baa-baa here and a baa-baa there. I can hardly remember what it's like. Sheep, for goodness' sake! But *you* don't need to be afraid of me, old friend. You're my pal."

"Afraid? Why would I be afraid of you?"

"Because I'm the Wolf and you're just a sheep. That might bother you."

Locke was incredulous. "Now I've heard everything. You're the Wolf and I'm 'just' a sheep? Karl, I'd never have thought you could say such a thing. Never! I thought we were friends. Though come to think of it, you did have a bit of this when you were a lamb . . . the others sometimes used to say: 'Oh, that Karl. You need to keep an eye on him. He really goes for it!' And René, he . . ."

"Oh, not René again." Karl spoke quietly, with a threatening undertone. "What about René?"

"That's what René said too, especially that time you pretended to be a vulture."

Karl was grinning now. "Thanks for reminding me. I think we need to pay our friend René a little visit. It's high time we put him in his place."

Karl was about to set off, but Locke held him back. "Wait. What are you doing? What do you want with René? You're the Wolf now. You must have more important things to do."

But Karl twisted away from him. "You keep your hooves off me. More important things to do? Like what? I'm the Wolf now. I've got to start somewhere, haven't I? This is our probationary period."

"Yes, that's true . . . but René? I like René. We were lambs together in the meadow."

"True. But that chapter's closed. I'm the Wolf, you're my right-hoof man, and René is a sheep. Come on."

Locke was still not sure. "But . . . Karl . . . you're surely not going to bite René in the leg?"

Karl grinned again. "Bite René in the leg? No, old friend, that's history. Don't you worry. We'll just pay him a little visit."

Locke was still not convinced. "Hmm . . . but . . . I still keep hearing 'we.' When *you're* the Wolf."

"That's what I keep telling you. I'm glad you've finally realized. Now come on."

And Karl set off with Locke trailing reluctantly behind.

Chapter 4

It was already dusk by the time they finally reached the edge of the large meadow. Karl hadn't been able to resist scaring the Three Little Pigs almost to death on the way. He had growled so menacingly that they had run off, squealing loudly.

Then one of them had fallen down. The other two had stumbled over him in their panic, and nothing could be seen but a quaking heap of tummies, ears, and curly tails. Karl had watched from behind a bush, highly amused. Now Karl and Locke were hiding in the brush, keeping watch for René.

"Look — there he is!" cried Locke.

"Excellent. Now, Locke, you go and tell him that I want to talk to him. He needs to come over here because I've got something to say to him."

"What do you want to say to him?"

"You can tell him I'm sorry; tell him I want to apologize, or something along those lines."

"Sorry? For what?"

"Well . . . back then . . . I might have been a bit too . . . enthusiastic . . ." Karl trailed off.

"Back then?"

"Well . . . the leg thing, you know . . ."

"So I was right! I suspected as much."

"Go on. Just tell him to come over here. I won't bite him."

"Are you sure?"

"Locke. Just get moving. You know me. I would never lie to you."

Locke was not entirely convinced. However, he left the thicket and stepped out into the meadow.

"René! Psst — René!"

René, busy with the grass, didn't immediately respond. He chewed slowly and carefully, then swallowed.

"René! It's me!"

René looked up. "Oh, it's you, Locke. Nice to see you."

"René . . . I . . . I mean, would you mind coming with me for a minute?"

"Why would I need to go anywhere at this time of day? In any case, I'm eating at the moment."

"Just come into the forest with me for a minute. Please."

"Into the forest? No thanks. Have you forgotten what we were told as lambs? *Avoid the forest in the night; for sheep it simply isn't right.* I'd rather stay here."

"But René, it's me, Locke."

"I know, I know. Long time no see, eh? Can't it wait until tomorrow? Why would I want to go into the forest? There isn't even anything decent to eat in there."

A powerful voice boomed from the forest.

"That's where you're mistaken. The forest is full of delicious herbs. You just need to know where to look for them. The wild benevolence of the forest. Come and taste it!"

René's ears pricked up. "Wait a minute . . . wasn't that Karl?"

"Yes it was," Locke replied.

"What's he doing here?"

"I . . . I mean, I think . . . he wants to apologize to you."

"Apologize? To me? Karl, of all sheep? Surely not."

"He wants to say he's sorry. For what happened before, you know, with your leg . . ."

"Ahh." René frowned. "And it's only just occurred to him to apologize now?"

"Better late than never. Come on. You're not normally like this."

"What's that supposed to mean?"

"Well . . . um . . . so petty. So unforgiving."

"I beg your pardon?" René said indignantly. "Petty? Me? I'm telling you, what happened wasn't funny. It really hurt."

"I don't think that's how he meant it. I think it was more of a joke."

"I don't believe this. A joke?" René was outraged now. "Karl bites me in the leg, and that's supposed to be a joke? And *I'm* the one who's petty and unforgiving? I don't believe this! It made me limp for nearly three weeks. I can do without jokes like that. And *you*, of all sheep . . . I'm surprised at you."

"What do you mean? What have I done?" Locke looked at René in astonishment. René was tugging at the grass. He looked up again. "Well . . ." René seemed distinctly sheepish now. "Well . . . you were always different from the others . . . yes, I know you've always hung around with that mutton-head, but you've always been different."

"What do you mean, different?"

"Just different. So . . . soft, somehow. So . . . fleecy. Rather like a . . . a cloud."

Locke swallowed. "Really? That's what you thought? That I was like a cloud?"

René nodded. "I still think so. Like a cloud in a blue summer sky."

Locke was speechless. He was like a cloud. Nobody had ever told him that before. "A cloud! René, I had no idea."

"Have you finished yet?" Karl's voice, which had initially sounded brusque and impatient, was now soft and pleasant. "Come on, René, old buddy. I'm really sorry. I didn't mean to do it — it was just a silly accident. Honest. We were all so young then. In any case . . . I've been suffering too. I lie awake at night feeling guilty. It's given me bad dreams. I'm always telling Locke how silly that business with you was. Isn't that right, Locke?"

Locke didn't reply.

"Come on, René," Karl wheedled. "I've got the tastiest grass here that I've ever seen in my life. I saved it especially for you. Come on, René — come and have supper with me."

René sighed. "Okay, if you insist. I really don't want to be petty and unforgiving." And René headed off toward the forest.

Locke, meanwhile, was whispering dreamily to himself, "I'm soft . . . I'm fleecy . . . I'm a cloud . . ."

He suddenly stopped short. "No! René, wait! René!"

Locke galloped off into the forest as quickly as he could. "René!"

But René had already disappeared into the thicket.

Chapter 5

It was dark in the forest. René cautiously set one hoof in front of the other, trying to spot his old playmate Karl as he did so. There was a stream nearby. René could hear it splashing softly. But however hard he tried, he couldn't see Karl's white fleece.

"Karl? Karl! Where are you?"

"Good evening, René."

René started. "Karl? Is that you?"

"Who else would it be?"

"But . . . Karl . . . I can't see you . . . not properly, I mean. Where are you?"

"Here, of course."

"But Karl . . . Karl doesn't look like that. You're not Karl! But your voice . . ."

"Aha. My voice."

"Karl is a sheep. With white fleece. But you . . ."

"What about me?"

"Your coat is black and bristly. You've got pointy ears, and your teeth . . . well, they're so sharp that you can't possibly eat grass. And they need cleaning, those teeth of yours. No, you're not Karl."

"Oh no? So who am I if I'm not Karl?"

"That voice . . . you're . . . an impostor. But . . ." René swallowed. "You are Karl. You're a sheep in wolf's clothing."

Karl laughed. "How very clever you are. That's precisely why you always annoyed me so much. Mr. Perfect Pupil. Mr. Know-It-All. But that's all history, and it's not going to help you one bit right now. And that's the end of it."

Horrified, René was rooted to the spot.

"But why . . ." He started again. "But what have I done to you?" he finally asked. "I never . . ."

Karl laughed again. A mocking laugh this time. "No, but *I* have. Oh, yes. I have. I bit you in the leg, and it was delightful. I could have eaten you up. And now I've come to claim the rest of you."

"Karl, for goodness' sake! What kind of nonsense is this? You're a sheep. Ridiculous fur coat or not, you're still a sheep. You can't do that. You're not a meat-eater. You'd get terrible indigestion. I wouldn't sit well in your stomach and you'd be blocked up for the rest of your life."

Karl was not impressed. "I know you and your smart-aleck remarks. Give it a rest. Sorry, old pal, but I need to get a move on. I'm still on probation." With these words, Karl took a massive leap and gobbled up René, fleece and all.

"Bleurgh!" He swallowed and choked. Then he took a deep breath and coughed.

At that moment, Locke came running up. "Where is he?"

"Who?" asked Karl.

"Who do you think? René, of course. Where is he?" demanded Locke. "René! René, where are you?"

"René, René, where are you?" Karl mimicked. "Where do you think he is? I'm the Wolf, René was a sheep . . . where do you think he is?"

Locke had to sit down. "*Was* a sheep? But Karl . . . that's impossible. You haven't . . . surely you haven't eaten him?"

"What else would I have done with him?"

"But Karl! I don't believe it. It's just not possible."

"Why isn't it possible? Of course it's possible. That's why they employed me, in case you've forgotten."

"But Karl, you're a sheep, and so is René. It's completely against nature."

Karl sighed. "Honestly, Locke, I don't see what your problem is. I'm the Wolf. He's a sheep. How many times do I have to tell you? I'm the eater and René's the meal. How is that against nature? That's what happens every day. All over the world."

"But not here! Not with you and René." Locke started bleating nervously to himself.

"Oh, stop making such a fuss, Locke," Karl snapped. "You knew full well what I was planning to do. I've got to prove myself — to show them what I'm made of. And you're my right-hoof man. I don't know what's the matter with you. It all went fine. Anyway, I'm tired. It's late." Karl yawned. "I'll eat a couple more of these tasty forest grasses; I'm sure they're good for the digestion. Then let's go to sleep. It's been a hard day. For you too."

But Locke still couldn't get his mind around it.

"How could you?"

"Do you mean practically speaking? Well, these fangs aren't bad. Though they're not that great for grass . . . I think I might skip this forest stuff and just settle down. He's lying terribly heavy in my stomach, that René. He did warn me, but I thought it was just him being a smart-aleck as usual."

Karl belched, then cautiously lowered himself to the ground. He lay on his side. With a satisfied look at his enormous belly he said, "Not bad for a first day's work, if you ask me. We're heading for great things. You'll see."

Locke shook his head. "You are mistaken. I'm not your right-hoof man; I'm a cloud."

But Karl didn't hear. He had already fallen asleep, and was snoring so loudly that the leaves above him were trembling.

Locke, however, couldn't settle. And that wasn't just because of the noise that Karl was making. He lay awake as everything churned around in his mind.

He suddenly jumped up. "That job center. That dwarf. It's all his fault."

He took a last look at the sleeping beast, then trotted hastily away.

Chapter 6

"Hello! Is anyone there? Hello! Someone must be there! Mr. Dwarf, Mr. Dwarf!" It was late, but Locke banged on the door all the same.

Eventually one of the windows was opened a crack.

"What on earth's going on? Stop that noise. Can't anyone get any peace around here?" The dwarf sounded sleepy and highly indignant.

"Please, please, open up. Quickly. It's important. He's eaten René! Open up!"

"Eaten René? So what? Ah . . . it's you. Hang on a moment."

The dwarf let Locke in.

"Go on then. What's the matter? Why all the racket?"

"Karl, I mean the Wolf, ate René. Gobbled him up. Just like that."

"Well, good for him. He's not wasting any time. Excellent. If he carries on like that, then there's no reason why he shouldn't get a permanent job. But couldn't this have waited until morning?"

"No! You're not getting the point. It's terrible. René is a friend. Karl should never have been allowed to do it. And now . . . we have to get René out again. Before he's digested. Right now!"

"Get René out again? *Get René out again?* What on earth are you talking about? If he's been eaten, he's been eaten. That's not my problem. And even if it were, what would you expect me to do about it? There's nothing I can do. I'm not allowed to get involved in things, no matter what. How about giving your friend a laxative: that would speed things up. Good night." The dwarf tried to turn away, but Locke clung to him.

"Hey! What do you think you're doing?" cried the dwarf.

"Isn't there anything else I can do?" Locke asked desperately. "I have to get René out as quickly as possible."

"This is getting ridiculous," snapped the dwarf as he freed his nightshirt from Locke's mouth. "As I have already told you, there's nothing I can do. Getting people out once they've been eaten is the Hunter's job. It doesn't have anything to do with me."

"Yes, that's it, the Hunter . . . where is he? I need to find him."

The dwarf shrugged regretfully. "There isn't a Hunter. The position's vacant at the moment." He pointed to a poster that was stuck to the wall behind his desk.

Locke read the words aloud. *"Hunter wanted. We need you! You must be firm and flexible, with a sense of justice and a steady hand. The successful applicant will be assertive and will welcome new challenges.* Okay then, if that's what it takes . . . I'd like the job."

"Oh, my giddy aunt. A job interview in the middle of the night! No way am I doing this. What on earth would happen if we all . . . Oh, all right, then. Come in. Take a seat."

The dwarf clambered onto his swivel chair and pulled out some papers. Locke chose to remain standing.

"Right. I understand that you want to become a Hunter. Good. What are your qualifications?"

"Quali . . . what?"

"Particular skills. Things that make you suitable for the Hunter job."

"I . . . um . . ." Locke thought frantically. Nothing immediately occurred to him. "I don't know . . . what sort of things do you mean? I'd just do it, whatever it is. And I can start immediately. I'm not afraid, and I'm strong . . ." He thought again. "And I can sew!" he burst out. "I like crafts. I used to sew the tails back on the lambs when they came a bit loose with all that wagging . . ." Locke looked hopefully at the dwarf.

"Crafts? Not exactly what I'd call a key qualification for becoming a Hunter."

"But surely there are lots of situations that involve cutting things open and sewing them up again?"

"Hmm. Maybe . . ." The dwarf was still not convinced.

"What about dealing with weapons?" he finally asked. "Any experience there?"

"Weapons?" Locke had to think hard. "You mean teeth? Hooves? Ear-splitting bleating?"

"No." The dwarf shook his head. "That's not what I mean. I mean arrows, rifles, poisoned apples — the usual stuff."

"No, I'm afraid not. But I'm a quick learner."

"Hmm. Right," said the dwarf. "In any case, now that I think about it, being good at crafts might not be such a bad

thing. I mean, our business favors the HFC method — in other words, the Hole-Free Coat method. It's proved very successful with regard to the durability of our clothing. Anyone can cut things open, but sewing them neatly back together again . . . yes, I like that idea. And how about your state of health? Is your blood pressure normal? Are you fit? Do you have a strong stomach? Can you bear the sight of blood?"

Locke took a deep breath. "Yes, I am completely healthy and I'm quite sure I'm fit for the job. And if I need to know how to shoot . . . as I said, I'm a quick learner."

"Hmm . . . well . . . if you say so. Given the particular circumstances, I'd be prepared to consider hiring you on a short-term basis."

Locke snorted with relief. "You're giving me the job. Thank you. *Thank you!* I'll start right away."

"Just a minute. Not so fast. There are some formalities first. Then there are a couple of things that you need. This all

has to be done properly. I don't want anyone to say afterwards that the job center didn't stick to the rules."

Locke began to paw the wooden floor impatiently with his front right hoof.

"If I might just ask you to stop doing that . . . Thank you so much. Right. I think we should agree on a probationary period here and now. Two days ought to be enough, I think . . . I've got other applicants ready and waiting. You're not the only one who wants this job. Here's some more information about the HFC method which I'd like you to read very carefully before you put it into practice."

He handed Locke a fat folder.

"There's a basic sewing kit included. I presumably don't have to tell you what to do with it. Then the rest of the equipment . . ." He stood up and opened the cupboard behind the swivel chair, just as he had done to get the wolf suit. This time he fetched out a long green cloak, a crushed felt hat, and an ancient rifle. "Here."

He handed Locke the cloak and hat. The cloak fit. It was a bit tight around the back, perhaps, but that didn't matter.

And as for the hat . . . well, he'd get used to it. "And now . . ."
Very carefully, the dwarf passed him the rifle. "Be careful with
it. It's an antique, and a bit tricky to use. To be honest, it
needs a complete overhaul. Only use it in a dire emergency,
and never — I mean never! — leave it lying around unse-
cured. And if innocent bystanders are harmed, then we accept
no responsibility."

Locke regarded the rifle with distaste. However, he gath-
ered everything together, pulled his hat down tightly over
his forehead, and went to the door. "Well, thank you and
goodbye."

"Just a moment. We'll meet again in two days' time. The day
after tomorrow. Look after things. Good luck, and . . ."

But Locke had already gone. He was galloping across the
fields and toward the forest as fast as his legs could carry him.

The dwarf tugged at his beard and yawned. "You can tell
that times are hard. You don't even get any peace at night. This
job isn't for me long-term. Maybe I'll go into mining, like my
brothers . . . you're the littlest one, they said, the job is ideal;
they'll believe anything you say. But I'm not so sure . . ."

Chapter 7

Although it was dark in the forest, Locke had no trouble finding Karl again. He just headed for the loud snoring. Karl was lying in the clearing exactly as Locke had left him an hour before. How long would it take for one sheep to digest another? However long, time was running out.

Karl was tossing and turning. He had removed his wolf's teeth before going to sleep and had placed them in the moss beside him.

For a moment Locke stood there like a statue. What now?

"Something's rummaging around in his stomach . . . thank God. That must mean that René is still alive. Well, I'm the Hunter. I'm the HUNTER," Locke muttered, spurring himself on. "That there is just a filthy wolf, that there is just . . . oh, Karl!" He tried once more. "That there is just a filthy wolf. I'm the Hunter. I slit the filthy creature's belly open and free his victim. Then I put a stone inside his stomach and sew him up again. That's the way it is. I'm the Hunter, and this here is the Wolf."

He put his sewing kit down on the ground. Then he looked around. "Right. I need a big stone."

Stones weren't a problem: there were plenty of them by the stream. Locke gazed at the sleeping Karl once more, then grasped the scissors firmly between his hooves. Then he took a deep breath and started to stab.

The fur was thick, and the leather was tough. Locke, in his heavy cloak, soon started to sweat, and his hooves started to hurt after just a couple of cuts. But he didn't give up. Lo and behold! René's head emerged through the slit into the fresh air, and he took a deep breath. The slit tore further; it was evidently not the first time that the fur coat had been cut open and sewn up again.

Locke tugged with all his might. Within moments, he had freed René from his tiny prison. René was now lying on the soft moss, gasping for air. Karl was still asleep. Or had he simply fallen unconscious?

Now came the hardest part. Locke had found a stone that looked as if it was about the right size. He tried to pick it up and put it inside the Wolf's stomach, but the stone was heavy and slippery, and Locke kept dropping it. "Come on — help me," he said to René; his voice was more commanding than

he had intended.

René was still on the ground, gasping. He looked up. "Oh! Mr. Hunter! Yes, of course, give me a moment, I'll be with you right away."

"This stone needs to go inside the Wolf's stomach."

"In his stomach? What on earth for?" René asked, baffled.

"Because . . . because that's just what you do." There was no time for long explanations. "That's the way it is. It has to be done properly."

René hurried to help the Hunter. Carefully, they slid the heavy stone into the Wolf's stomach. Then they set about sewing it back up. Locke threaded the needle and gave René his instructions.

"Right. Pull the fur tight and press the two edges together so I can sew them up. Tighter. Tighter! Yes. That's it. Thank you." Locke started to sew the Wolf's stomach up with big stitches.

René looked at him closely. Then all of a sudden he said, "Mr. Hunter. No offense, but you look somehow familiar . . . might we have met before somewhere?"

Locke quickly pulled his hat further down over his fore-

head. "Be quiet. I need to concentrate. Thank you . . . that'll do. I can finish off on my own. You go down to the stream and give yourself a good wash. You stink."

René was about to protest, but instead trundled off to the stream. Locke had only just finished his final stitch when René returned, sopping wet. "Finished already?"

René watched Locke bite the thread off with his teeth. "Mr. Hunter, you really do remind me a lot of . . ."

"Of?"

"You remind me of . . ." René sniffed the air and took a cautious step toward Locke.

"That smell . . . I know that smell. Mr. Hunter, you're Locke! No doubt about it. You're Locke!"

At that moment, Karl began to toss and turn again.

"I feel sick," he groaned. "And my stomach . . . what's wrong with my stomach . . . ow . . . Locke. Locke! I'm sick, Locke, where are you? I'm so thirsty . . . I need a drink . . . and my fur . . . what's happened to my fur? It's far too tight!"

He tugged at his wolf's coat, but he was stuck tight in it. "Locke, Locke, where are you? I feel so sick . . . I've never felt so sick in all my life . . . there was a stream somewhere around

here . . . I have to have a drink. Locke, where are you?"

Locke didn't reply. He and René had retreated, and were watching Karl as he staggered to his feet and stumbled off toward the stream.

"What's wrong with my stomach?" groaned Karl. "I mean . . . I can hardly move . . . Hey!" There was a loud splash. Then a gurgling sound. "I . . . what's going on . . . Help! Help! I'm drowning! I . . ." Then came the gurgling sound again.

"He's fallen into the stream!" René set off at a run. Locke followed him reluctantly.

"Locke, Locke, help me . . ." Karl's voice was already fainter.

"Locke! Hurry!" cried René. "He's drowning. You have to help me!"

Locke had by now reached the stream and was watching René trying in vain to pull Karl out of the cold water. He had evidently lost consciousness again.

"I'm not Locke. I'm the Hunter. This here is the filthy Wolf. Everything's just as it should be, and that's why . . ."

"For goodness' sake, stop talking and help me," René cried. "Have you all gone crazy? Take off those horrible rags and grab hold of him. You're Locke. You're not a hunter — you're a cloud. Come on!"

"I'm a cloud?" Locke repeated, astonished.

Then, as if he had suddenly awakened from a dream, he cast off his cloak and hat, sprang towards the stream, and helped René drag Karl onto the bank.

Chapter 8

Karl was lying motionless on the grass before them.

René bent over him, listening carefully.

"He's still alive," he said, relieved. "Presumably just un-conscious again."

"Why are you so bothered about him?" Locke asked. "Given that he did such a terrible thing to you."

René shrugged. "I can't just stand by and watch while an old pal drowns. Even if that old pal just happens to be a real jerk. But never mind. Everyone else can be bananas as long as I'm not. Thanks for helping me. I'd never have managed it on my own."

Locke was embarrassed. "Well . . . I had to. You're right. But he . . . and the Hunter . . ."

"Yes, I know. The Big Bad Wolf and the Hunter . . . that old story. Thanks for getting me out," said René, turning

slightly red.

"No need to thank me for that," said Locke.

"Oh yes there is."

"So?" asked Locke. "What now?"

René laughed. "What do you think? We have to get that pesky stone out. And I've got an idea. Pass me the scissors. It'll be a great pleasure, cutting open this stomach again."

Locke handed the scissors to him. Together, they pulled the stone out of the Wolf's stomach. Then René undid his ribbon with its bell, took the bell off, and cradled it in his hooves for a moment. Then he laughed. He bent down over Karl's stomach so that Locke couldn't see what he was doing. "Come on, then. Stitch him up!"

Locke got out his needle and thread once more and began to sew. What on earth had René wanted the bell for? Then he heard a faint jingling sound coming from Karl's stomach.

"Don't tell me you put the bell . . ."

"Of course I did," René replied gleefully. "So much for bell-wearers! He won't forget that in a hurry."

Locke had to laugh. Then he quickly finished his sewing. "That's it for today. We'll take this bell-wearing Wolf back to his boss tomorrow."

They looked at one another, exhausted but satisfied.

And before very long, they were both fast asleep.

Chapter 9

The next morning, they were awakened by the sound of miserable groaning. "Locke . . . Locke . . . for goodness' sake, Locke, wake up. I feel so sick . . ."

Locke staggered to his feet. His legs didn't seem to want to cooperate just yet. He made his way stiffly over to Karl. "What's the matter?"

"Locke, I feel dreadful. The outside of my stomach hurts, and I feel sick inside . . . could you give me a sip of water?"

Locke filled the water bottle that had come with the Hunter's costume and took it over to him. Karl emptied it greedily. Locke watched closely as Karl took a swig and the water ran down his throat and . . . thank goodness. The stitches held. They were watertight.

"Locke . . . I . . . I think I'll just lie here for a while. I know it's silly, given that I'm still on probation. But I . . ." He groaned again. "Locke, to be honest . . . I'm not sure I'm the right man for the job. It somehow doesn't agree with me. Eating René was fine; he's a pain in the neck and he got what

he deserved. But all the same . . . so much meat at one time doesn't agree with me. The very thought of it . . . the seven little goats. And an entire grandmother . . ." Karl rolled his eyes. "Just thinking about it is enough to make me sick. And what's more, this fur coat itches like crazy!"

He looked down at himself. "My poor stomach . . . I wonder how long it will take for me to digest René? Am I really going to be blocked up for the next hundred years? Hello!" He paused, listening carefully. "What on earth's that? A bell . . . ?"

Meanwhile René had gotten up too. "What's what? Some kind of digestive problem? Well . . . don't blame me!"

Karl stared at him. "René! What are you doing here? How . . . ?"

"Who knows?" René laughed sweetly. "A hunter, perhaps? What do you think, Locke?"

"A hunter?" Karl said, astonished. "You mean . . . there just happened to be . . . a hunter? Well, hunter or no hunter," Karl paused briefly, "René, I'm glad you're out. And . . . I'm sorry, René."

"What for?"

"For what I did to your leg. I did mean to do it, but now I'm sorry. Truly."

"Ah." René gave him a long look.

Karl swallowed. "And that business yesterday . . . um . . . , I'm sorry for that too. But . . . I don't know what happened . . . I really wasn't myself. It was the Wolf who did it."

Locke couldn't help himself. "Oh, here we go!" he burst out. "You just stop your bleating. The Wolf did it? Yeah, right. Who was in that wolf suit? You. *You* were the Wolf. You and nobody else."

"Well, um, yes," Karl admitted. "But . . . you probably can't imagine how different everything suddenly looks once you're wearing a wolf suit. Try it on if you don't believe me!"

Locke was silent. The way he had felt in the Hunter's costume was still fresh in his mind.

"No," he said finally. "You take off that suit. It needs to be returned as quickly as possible. You lie right here and don't move an inch."

"Fine. If you say so."

Karl did as he was told, then lay down again. "But . . . what's that?"

"What's what?"

"Listen." Karl moved cautiously. There was a faint tinkling sound. "That ringing . . . it seems almost as if it were coming from my stomach."

René grasped his neck. "My bell! My bell must still be in your stomach. Oh no!"

"What? Your bell in my stomach? I can't stand it. I can't bear the sound of bells! How on earth am I going to get it out again?"

"Hmm . . ." René seemed to be thinking. "Locke, didn't we see a pair of sharp scissors lying around? They ought to do the trick. Okay, Karl, you lie down and we'll just . . ."

Karl groaned. "Sharp scissors? Lie down? Thanks — but no way. I'm feeling a bit sensitive in that area at the moment."

"But Karl . . . you with a bell!" René shook his head. "I really can't imagine that one. But it's up to you. Come on, Locke, let's go."

As they left, he turned back once more. "Oh, and there's just one more thing, Karl. That vulture act of yours? It's curtains, once and for all."

"Oh come on," said Karl. "I said I was sorry."

"You just don't get it, do you!" grumbled René.

"Yes, okay, okay. Keep your fleece on. I get it. And anyway, we've outgrown that stuff, haven't we, René?"

And Karl shut his eyes.

Chapter 10

The dwarf was anything but pleased to see them returning so soon together with all their gear.

"Back already? Didn't we say the day after tomorrow?"

"Yes, we did. But you need to understand that this job just isn't our cup of tea. We don't think we're up to it. We're sorry."

"You could have thought of that beforehand. And . . . my lovely wolf suit!" The dwarf was indignant. "What on earth were you thinking? I can't accept it back in that condition."

The two sheep didn't seem particularly contrite.

"You know," René finally said, "I'm afraid you have no choice. And if you look closely, you'll see that it's already been stitched up several times in the same place.

Maybe a zipper . . ."

"A zipper?" blustered the dwarf. "Are you kidding? A zipper would ruin the whole effect. But on the other hand . . . " His expression brightened. "It would make the wolf suit last longer. I think I'll revisit that when I get a moment. Good day to you!"

Outside, the two sheep looked at one another. René cautiously touched his friend's curly fleece with his hoof.

"I knew it. Soft, like a cloud."

"You really think so?" asked Locke.

"Of course. Like a thundercloud."

And, laughing, they frolicked away across the meadow.

The dwarf, however, was putting his posters back up. There was an extra one. It said: *Job Center Manager Vacancy.* His mining gear was already waiting for him in the corner.